S·T·A·R·D·I·N·E·S
SWIM HIGH ACROSS THE SKY
and other poems

* * * * *

by **JACK PRELUTSKY**

illustrated by **CARIN BERGER**

GREENWILLOW BOOKS
An Imprint of HarperCollinsPublishers

To VAD for your leap of faith, to BB for every little thing,
to Joseph Cornell (of course!), and, as always, to Thea
—C. B.

Stardines Swim High Across the Sky and Other Poems
Text copyright © 2012 by Jack Prelutsky
Illustrations copyright © 2012 by Carin Berger

The miniature dioramas in this book are assemblages created using a
combination of cut paper, found ephemera, vintage engravings (which
were scanned, manipulated in Photoshop, and then printed out), beeswax,
wire, thread, and wood. Once each piece was made, it was then photographed
digitally to prepare the full-color art.

The text type is Courier.
Photography by Porter Gillespie

Library of Congress Cataloging-in-Publication Data

Prelutsky, Jack.
Stardines swim high across the sky and other poems
by Jack Prelutsky ; illustrations by Carin Berger.
                    p. cm.
               "Greenwillow Books."
ISBN 978-0-06-201464-1 (trade bdg.)—ISBN 978-0-06-201465-8 (lib. bdg.)
[1. Imaginary creatures—Juvenile poetry. 2. Children's poetry, American.]
            I. Berger, Carin, ill. II. Title.
      PS3566.R36S73 2012 811'.54—dc23 2011025993
              19 20 21 SCP 10 9 8 7 6 5 4
                    First Edition

 Greenwillow Books

For Madelyn and Thomas
—J. P.
With great gratitude
to Porter
—C. B.

CONTENTS

StARDiNEs

STARDINES swim high across the sky,
And brightly shine as they glide by.
In giant schools, their brilliant lights
Illuminate the darkest nights.
            /////
When other creatures are in bed,
STARDINES still twinkle overhead.
In silence, these nocturnal fish
Are set to grant the slightest wish.

STAR-deens

B L U F F A L O E S are bulky beasts,
Preposterously large.
Their demeanor is imposing,
They appear to be in charge.

     *   *   *

Despite their size and attitude,
They're neither fierce nor tough,
And B L U F F A L O E S just run away
If you should call their bluff.

               /////

BLUFF-a-lows

SWAP-uh-teez

SwAPitIs

S W A P I T I S meet every day
To put their goods out on display.
No sooner have they set up shop,
Than S W A P I T I S begin to swap.
They've all amassed assorted things,
Like tennis racquets with no strings,
Like busted bikes, old moldy boots,
And out-of-fashion three-piece suits.

S W A P I T I S have endless stocks
Of worn-out socks and broken clocks,
Of warped guitars, chipped bongo drums,
And slightly cracked aquariums.
Back and forth within the woods
They trade for one another's goods,
Exchanging wingless model planes
For misassembled plastic trains.

They barter dented baseball bats
For oddly decorated hats,
For unattractive broken beads,
Or rusty tools that no one needs.
At dusk, when it's too dark to see,
They pack their wares reluctantly
And wish they didn't have to stop,
For S W A P I T I S just love to swap.

ChOrMOranTs

CHORMORANTS are busy birds
That toil from sun to sun.
They labor over senseless chores
They're certain must be done.
They work at this, they work at that,
And never think to ask
If they accomplish anything
With any pointless task.

CHORMORANTS are serious
And have no use for jest.
They feel it is their destiny
To rarely ever rest.
They're strangers to frivolity
And neither sing nor dance.
Their days are endless drudgery—
Poor boring CHORMORANTS.

*　*　*

Fig. 64.

CHORE-mor-ants

FOUNTAIN

LION

FOUNTAIN LIONS, lithe and lean,
Add gaiety to any scene.
The only lions no one dreads,
They all have fountains on their heads.
They are not predatory beasts
Upon the prowl for easy feasts.
Instead, with evident delight,
They run their fountains day and night.

Of course, they have to drink and drink
To keep those fountains in the pink.
When water is in short supply,
Those FOUNTAIN LIONS soon run dry.
But, as a rule, they drink their fill,
Then spout with artistry and skill.
At sending up an aqueous stream,
FOUNTAIN LIONS reign supreme.

*   *   *

FOUN-tin lions

SLOBSTERS

SLOBSTERS are slovenly,
SLOBSTERS are crude.
SLOBSTERS love mashing
And smushing their food.
Their sense of decorum
Is woefully small.
SLOBSTERS don't have
Many manners at all.

                               *   *   *

SLOBSTERS don't seem
To be happy unless
They're dropping their supper
And making a mess.
They're simply so sloppy
We have to conclude
That SLOBSTERS are slovenly,
SLOBSTERS are crude.
        /////

SLOBSTERS

SLOB-stirs

PLAN-duz

PLaNdaS

PLANDAS sit around all day,
Planning what to do.
Their plans amount to nothing,
For they never see them through.
They plan to run a marathon
Or take a railroad trip.
They plan to cross the ocean
On a wooden sailing ship.

*

*

*

They plan to learn to roller-skate,
To juggle, and to fence.
They plan to go to clown school
And cavort in circus tents.
They plan to play the saxophone
And form their own brass bands. . . .
But PLANDAS never do these things—
They just keep making plans.

JoLLyFiSh

JOLLYFISH are radiant,
Ebullient blobs of mirth,
With merry dispositions
From the moment of their birth.
Though they know their every motion
Is dependent on the tides,
They laugh with such abandon
That they almost split their sides.

* * *

Their humor is infectious,
And as aimlessly they drift,
Their buoyant effervescence
Gives the neighborhood a lift.
JOLLYFISH possess the gift
Of fundamental glee—
There's no creature half as happy
At the bottom of the sea.

JOH-lee-fish

ThE SoBCat

The SOBCAT is sad / That miserable SOBCAT's
As a feline can be / Been moaning for years,
And spends its time crying / Sitting alone,
Continuously. / Weeping copious tears.
It has no real reason / Because it delights
To be so morose. / In its own misery,
It's simply its nature / The SOBCAT is sad
To act lachrymose. / As a feline can be.

SOB-cat

MaGPiPEs

MAGPIPES sound unpleasant—
They've a tendency to drone.
Their voices are a nasal,
Cacophonic monotone.
They self-inflate their feathered chests
Until they're filled with air,
Then on and on those noisy birds
Monotonously blare.
/////
Nothing but a MAGPIPE
Likes the sounds a MAGPIPE makes.
At best you can describe them
As unmusical mistakes.
Don't listen to a MAGPIPE
If you have another choice.
Consider yourself lucky
If you never hear its voice.
* * *

MAG-pipe

TAT-ul-snake

TATTLESNAKE

TATTLESNAKE

TATTLESNAKE,
TATTLESNAKE,
Overly keen
To tattle repeatedly—
Truly you're mean.
You're nosy, annoying,
You're venomous, vile.
You don't mind your business,
We don't like your style.

TATTLESNAKE,
TATTLESNAKE,
Making us moan,
Tattling all day,
Leaving no one alone.
Why must you tattle,
And what makes you feel
That anyone cares
About things you reveal?

TATTLESNAKE,
TATTLESNAKE,
Acting so wrong,
Sticking your snout
Where it doesn't belong.
We think your comeuppance
Is long overdue
And hope someday soon
Someone tattles on you.

* * *

B R A I N D E E R are very clever,
B R A I N D E E R are very wise.
Their brains are very wrinkled
And of a massive size.
Their minds are overflowing
With extreme intelligence.
B R A I N D E E R have lots of knowledge,
B R A I N D E E R have lots of sense.
            *   *   *
With endless perseverance
They serenely mill about,
Reflecting on the universe
And figuring it out.
But, sadly, they cannot convey
A solitary thought,
For B R A I N D E E R cannot speak nor write—
Their thinking is for naught.
                    / / / / /

BRAIN-deer

ThE
GLOOse

The GLOOSE may be the weirdest bird + The GLOOSE is so adhesive
That ever took to wing. + That to free it from its plight
It has an odd propensity + Requires a lot of people
To stick to anything. + Pulling with a lot of might.
It often backs into a tree + Sometimes it takes a football team
And instantly adheres, + To pry the creature loose.
So then it honks and honks and honks + The conclusion's inescapable—
Till help at last appears. + It's hard to be the GLOOSE.

GLOOSE

PANTEATER

PANTEATERS eat pants
Anytime, anywhere.
The cloth doesn't matter—
PANTEATERS don't care.
On trousers of cotton,
Silk, linen, or wool,
PANTEATERS keep chewing
Until they are full.

They eat polyester
And nylon with zest.
There's no single fabric
PANTEATERS like best.
They gnaw every pocket
And belt loop and cuff.
It often takes hours
Till they've had enough.

Their diet's unchanging,
Except for dessert,
For then they may tackle
A sweater or shirt.
But most of the time,
If they have half a chance,
PANTEATERS eat nothing
But mountains of pants.

PANT-ee-ters

WEDGEHOGS are triangular.   *   WEDGEHOGS, when they wander,
WEDGEHOGS are benign.   *   Never wander very far.
WEDGEHOGS are considerate.   *   WEDGEHOGS always feel at home
WEDGEHOGS wait in line.   *   Exactly where they are.

WEDGE-hogs

* 3 3 *

BaRDvaRkS

BARDVARKS think they're poets
And persist in writing rhyme.
Their words are uninspired
And a total waste of time.
But BARDVARKS do not know this,
So not only do they write
With unbearable pretension—
They incessantly recite.

* BARDVARKS have no talent
For composing simple verse.
* They don't improve with practice
And in fact are getting worse.
* Undeterred, they keep on writing
And reciting every day.
* That's why BARDVARKS are a problem—
* You can't make them go away.

BARD-varx